Withdrawn

WALT DISNEY's
Pinocchio and the Whale

By Gina Ingoglia
Illustrated by Phil Ortiz
and Diana Wakeman

A GOLDEN BOOK • NEW YORK
Western Publishing Company, Inc., Racine, Wisconsin 53404

Geppetto makes toys
out of wood.
He makes one toy that
looks like a small boy.

"I will call you
Pinocchio,"
says Geppetto.
"You are a nice toy.
But I wish I had a
real boy!"

The Blue Fairy hears Geppetto
make his wish.
"I will make you walk
and talk,"
she tells Pinocchio.
She waves her wand.

"I can walk and talk!"
says Pinocchio.
"Am I a real boy?"
"No," says the Blue Fairy.
"You are still made of wood.

"You have to be good,"
the Blue Fairy tells
Pinocchio.
"Then I will make you
into a real boy.

"Meet Jiminy,"
says the Blue Fairy.
"He will help you."
"I will help you
to be good,"
says Jiminy.

But Pinocchio meets
some bad boys.
He runs away with them.
The bad boys and Pinocchio
start to grow donkey ears
and donkey tails.
"You have been bad,"
says Jiminy.

"I want to be good,"
says Pinocchio.
"I will go back home."

But no one is home!
Geppetto is away.
Pinocchio finds a letter.
It is from Geppetto.

Jiminy reads the letter.
"Pinocchio," says Jiminy.
"Geppetto went to look
for you in his boat.
But Monstro the whale
ate the boat!
Now Geppetto is inside
the whale!"

11

"A whale ate Geppetto!"
cries Pinocchio.
He runs away from Jiminy.

"Come back!" calls Jiminy.
"I am going to find Monstro,"
says Pinocchio.

Pinocchio and Jiminy
see lots of water.
"Monstro is out there,"
says Pinocchio.
"I am going to jump
into the water!"

Pinocchio jumps into the water.
Jiminy jumps in with him.

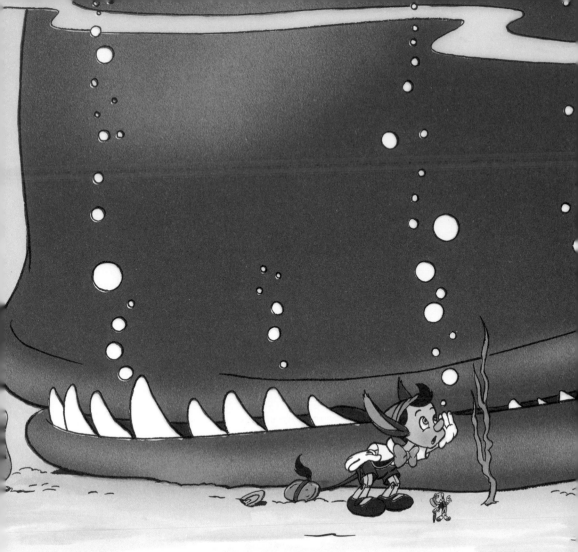

They look for Monstro.
"There he is!"
yells Pinocchio.
Monstro is asleep.
"Wake up!" calls Pinocchio.

"What if Monstro hears you
and wakes up?"
asks Jiminy.
"Then I will go inside and get
Geppetto out," says Pinocchio.

Monstro wakes up!
He does not see
Pinocchio and Jiminy.
But he does see
some nice fish.

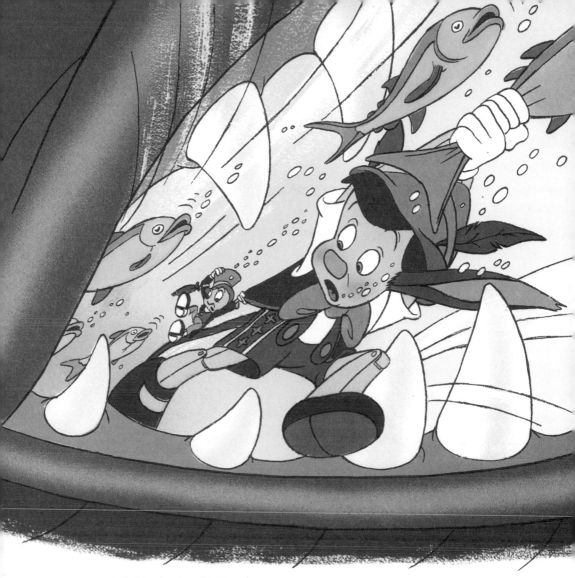

The big whale eats
the fish up.
Whoosh!
Pinocchio and Jiminy
go inside with the fish.

Geppetto is fishing
from his boat.
Geppetto pulls up a fish.

Now he pulls up another fish—
and Pinocchio!
"Pinocchio!" cries Geppetto.
"Father, I am here to get you out!"
says Pinocchio.

"I will make a big fire," Pinocchio tells Geppetto. "The fire will make lots of smoke. The smoke will make Monstro sneeze.

When Monstro sneezes,
we can get out."
Geppetto helps Pinocchio
make a fire out of wood.

The smoke makes Monstro
sneeze a BIG sneeze!
"Here we go," says Pinocchio.

"We are going out."

"I am so happy," says Geppetto.

"Now we can go home."

But Monstro finds
Geppetto and Pinocchio.

"Look out!" yells Geppetto.
"Jump into the water!"
yells Pinocchio.

Geppetto starts to sink.
"I will save you,"
says Pinocchio.
"Hang on!"

Geppetto is washed ashore.
He is safe.
Pinocchio is lying
in the water.
He is not moving.
"My son, my son,"
cries Geppetto.
"You were so brave."

Geppetto carries his son home.

He puts Pinocchio on the bed.
The Blue Fairy comes.
"You have been very good,"
she says to Pinocchio.
"You saved Geppetto.
I will make you
into a real boy."

And the Blue Fairy
makes Pinocchio
into a real boy at last!
Pinocchio, Geppetto, and
Jiminy live happily ever after.